Daughter's Diary of Poetry

2022

SONYA JOHNSTON

Daughter's Diary of Poetry
Copyright © 2022 by Sonya Johnston

Tellwell Talent
www.tellwell.ca

ISBN
978-0-2288-7329-7 (Hardcover)
978-0-2288-7328-0 (Paperback)

I would like to acknowledge my brothers and sisters for encouraging me, especially my youngest sister for being the driving force behind me. My beloved Mother who believed in me and my husband who made it happen.

I dedicate this book to my daughter
Naomi Bernice Marie Godin
Aug 03, 1984 - April 06, 2018

Preface

This is a compilation of Christian and secular poetry. Though I compiled it from different events in my life, it would be my hope that the reader would see it in light of their own lives. I hope it is a blessing to you.

I've grown

Sorrow visits awaiting my grief
come they do they come as a thief,
what shall I say betrayal gains another day.
She looks and says come lets pray-
she is more clever than I,
smiling she grins and says.......we're all going to die
I come as always and my hate has grown.
My desire is set, this time I'll wage a bet-
I'll welcome your husband and say it is you
he doesn"t care he needs a ticket too.
I did it before with you and your wife,
I even got you to end your life.
You wouldn't die as I'd wished...........
so I devised another plan and this time your sure to
understand, and you will not know what's in my
other hand.

Sincerely yours

I heard with no ears, I crept with no legs
I felt with no needs and hurt with no heart
I felt with no touch, I wept with no tears and
I gasped with no breath.
I sighed with no fear, I saw with no eyes -
I come with no meaning, I speak with no voice.
I laughed with no happiness -
I looked up to no sky and down to no ground,
I came with no warning and nothing I found.
The price to pay to know oneself, sitting alone
upon that shelf,
to know nothing......nothing at all and still be able
to stand that tall.

Please allow me to introduce my daughter,
allow me to share with you her laughter - be
cause today that all changed.
She stopped laughing and I stopped asking.
She stopped planning and hoping - I stopped
waiting.
Today my daughter stopped breathing and I
stopped living.

Tempt me not

Sin - how great you are, shine on me oh sin
that I might see your glory.....
Express yourself in earthly language,
that I may understand you.
Let me know oh sin.....let me know you
through and through, let there be no place
in me that you haven't touched oh sin.
How great you are in all your glory,
tempt me not.
I have drunken deep of your well, I have
counted the sin as numerous as the grains
of sand on the beach.
Still - I thirst and I hunger,
for - you sin have forsaken me.
Everytime I drink of your waters, I drink deep-
but your wells have dried, leaving me tired and
weary eyed.
I look around and I see a cup, all I have to do
is look up - in my esteem I take careful aim,
knowing that sin is waiting to blame.
Water flowed from a water spout-
casting sin out, it was overflowing and I recieved
my first knowing.

Who am I...............

I am sand without it's beach and water without
it's formula. I am a blade of grass without it's edge.
a fever without it's virus and a flower without it's stem.
I am dirt without it's ground - I am feet without it's toes
and hands without it's arms.
I am charm without it's influence and gain without it's
miles. I am journey without it's road and a jar with
out it's substance. I am a plant without it's roots- a
toil within with no regard, a fool of fights with no anger.
I am a stake with no challenge, a mole without it's
birthday. I am a snake without it's belly - a tree without
it's holly and a berry without it's seed.
I am ground warfare with no enemy, I am a thorn bush
with no prickles.
Who am I...........
I am a mug without the filling, a cut without the wound.
I am branches without the trunk and an iron without
the board.
My name is empty and I'm always full.

Wanna know

I don't care if it's dry, wet- boiling or set
I'm never going to forget.

Sonya Johnston

Don't show me

~~~~~~

The sand storms have shown me up
and the quick sand has swallowed me whole,
nevertheless there is still something that I
want you to know.
The sand storm in the bottle and my hand
on the throddle-
the machine doesn't move, it's really not
in the groove.
Iv'e taken it's place and my shoes have no
lace- keep up to me I'm at your pace.
Don't show me nothing;
I already ran the race, it's not about me
I already dealt the ace.
I lament for the people, a remnant of the
steeple.
My pride - I hide deep inside, my ego....I let you go,
my selfish ways....it's of those days- a day not
numbered or sown, something I should have known.
So little to know and now I have to go.
Blessings in all your ways, may it go before you all
your days.
May the sun never go down on your anger, casteth
me not away oh Lord and let your wrath not rain
down on me.
~~~~~~

I love you mom, never worry about me
and never count another day that I am gone.
Don't give yourself another reason where you
went wrong.
Mom please don't cry over another song,
please mom you know I'm strong.
I love you mom, now you be strong.

Lets not pretend

Here I sit before a door, I thrust it open and slip on the floor - not a creature is stirring not even the poor.

I thump it a little but it looks rather brittle, I move to the left and then to the right hoping no one is in sight.

The rest of my life

The darkness over shadows me, it consumes me
by night - today I spend the rest of my life living
a book of a man with no wife, a life lived by the
edge of a knife; blistering and forbidden - the
darkness descends into a catastrophic event.

Living by the river in a canvas tent where daily meditations
are carelessly spent, I was spiraling downward with
the wrong intent and another night came and went.

Another dark night came to threaten my life,
oh how the darkness does over shadow me -
consuming me by night - forboding every light.

Zoning

I'll zone in on it tonight, a fixed
generation - they scream all night.
Regarding the end, please.... lets
not pretend.
So scratch your head and pretend
your dead - at the end of the day
gather and pray.

The silent whisper

To profound are the words of a troubled heart the silent
whisper is heard from miles apart, can you not see the
depth of my heart - where years have tainted every part.
Seek me not - oh my deep, into my fine
frame work.......so incomplete.
I'll walk along with you on that trail after
giving birth at the alter of frail.
Oh destiny........come work with me and see what we
can be. My own down-syndrome anti-dote to every
problem, in a heartful of troublesome stories, I have
given a handful of posies.......counting on seeing
His face, oh Lord grant me a little more grace.

Just for a day

When I said I was sorry it wasn't for just a day,
while the priest in his garnments hung in a lowly
way. To offer my life at the table, for my family
I am more than able. To forsake my will.. it is my flesh
I would have to kill. The agony.. I was fitted with
jester instead, I hungered and was not fed. To be rich
is the beginning of my failure, but my rich - in heart,
is the beginning of yours. An apology is forever, let
me stand correct and this day rather let me be direct.
Like a smoke house I give my offering - the first fruits
of my labors, careful not to offend my neighbors. The
harvest is ripe, a calling of my type. Silence all the
gain seekers and I'm leaving all the speakers, I take
nothing with me but my song in hand; I'm off to meet
the Lord in the stormy sand. Don't try and stop me..
no don't you dare, or of the Lord really be ware. I
sing my song as I enter in, I am here.. here to win.
My days are dark and my groans unheard,
a place where I'm as blind - as my heart is
sore, so deep within I settle the score.
I go solo in my soul, I walk alone.. but I walk whole. Oh
Lord how much you must see, so very far beyond me. I
want to touch the light.. I want to break through the night.

A second in........

My intense passion......for the after thought of such an occassion - the passed on word of revelation; I've etched the circumstances far beyond my own reach. I had a dream of a girl - then darkness befell the country with a swirl. I could see but with one eye and judgement birthed - it was very nigh. I reached beyond the stars and found a rainbow; far reaching what I'd ever know, but one I didn't need - nevertheless I count it as my treasures deed......so help me I have planted my heavenly seed.

Sonya Johnston

Afraid....

Every day was afraid.....it was afraid of the dark it
was afraid that it would even take the mark. It was
afraid of the light and even that it might. Every day
feared the weak and went on a winning streak, there
he welcomed the meek - but feared the strong for so
very long. It feared empty - for it was full of plenty.

A little conditioning

Bitter sweet we shall never meet, be it
a day that I would greet, as though we
would meet. Have it not on ice- as it was,
rather past is more at a welcome- at last
Bitter sweet let us not meet, impressions on
my feet, make it ice cold......forgetting the heat
lest we meet. At the corridor it was one and all,
so take my hand oh Lord- I'm so very small
I'm wrapped around the lamp post and feeling
a bit like the host- that's when I sung a song,
I sang it from on deep, deep in my sleep. I
hummed along while I sang my song, from deep-
so deep in my sleep. I heard a groan, a groan
from on deep; a groan that would lead me home,
home to the place of the heart- a heart that knows the
home....the home that did groan. A groan from on deep,
deep within the soul- a soul that only I did know.

Un – announced

Lost in our souls and announced a little too late
last call, they've shut the gate. Wiery we are, lost
in the dark - the last of us is guided to the park. I
shutter at the sights that they see through the lights.
It won't be long, tis far.. I'll be answering that
phone. Near is the fate that good old pearly gate.

Myself / inner nature

A pair of pajamas I sent you two, I didn't get them new but I knew that didn't matter much to you. I dressed you like a cougar and candy kisses that dressed you up. Sleep oh so peacefully honey and sleep like you have lots of money, be cozy and warm like the season wrapped you in itself - never sit your life on that self there's oh so much to yourself. Remember me sweet pea as I remember your laughter....now and ever after. Let me run this ship and I'll run it for a while just because I want to see you smile, Never look back it's something you'll never track and forget the past, at last.........at last. Oh sweet heart we are so many miles apart, how long will you be away - there are things I've forgotten to say. I don't know where you went or how far you were sent, I just know a thousand paces or a thousand laces, what does it matter at a yard away and no reason to stay. Heaven is a place for little girls, far as expected to be dressed in curls and heaven is a place for young women, where you are dressed in fine white linen. Today is the first day of every day of my life and I know that today is my first day and yesterday was my last - though count it not as my past, at last........ at last. The warmth that falleth upon my brow drippeth like the dew drops, one by one until the sun has come. I desert myself seeking shelter as a bird does fly, I confess oh raven I soar so high, I seek comfort under your wings while I sort out some things. The lie of my soul and the sweet, sweet song of being whole.

Sonya Johnston

Mother............

A mother's love is undying, unwavering and everlasting.
It is unconditional and strong and her patience and
suffering are long - it endureth to the end and it will
never pretend but always true and always real.
A mothers arms are tender and giving, they don't
weaken or give out - they are good and strong - holding
her child long, they will be there when the flood
comes in, showing you always that you can win.

So soon.............

Sweet surrender you were due in september, with the fall leaves and the september breeze - it left little to grieve..............so three weeks early and my bundle arrived. Sweet surrender, I had you before september. I could have died, you were so wide eyed, and us - we couldn't decide. Sweet surrender - I'm never going to forget her.

Sonya Johnston

I live with it

I lead you into a place my dear, forgive me.. I lead you
into a place of fear. It was the road to danger - so few
take as it leads only to anger. You were my little fawn
and so eager.. like lazarus, their left overs so meager.
There was a stranger in the church, I sat every week and
listened to him until I'd seen the wolf and his chinny,
chin, chin. There was a station - two sisters of the same;
they treated you in this way, but it was only a game. The
station was full of unusual debre' and a group of vagabons
were coming to greet me. The sisters killeth me with
their panting words, they did their best; with no more
than a kitten apart - I thrust one more in the heart. I
dawn a new day never looking their way and the group
of vagabons walked my way. Say it's forever and long for
me never, together we are as one - united and done.
The Lord is my savoir, my God and my hope. He is
the eagle with the nest, where we can run and find
rest. So let us not grow wiery and let our thoughts
remain close to him. Lately we've been dwelling with
a lot of hope and we've been shown a wide scope
and in so seeing we now know how to cope.

Pine needle

Pine needle has left me again, left me pining for the
end, it's my juresdiction so I just pretend and redeemed
by fiction to the end. I've got a finger or two left and
I know where I stand cleft. Could you tell pine needle
I'm at the billards, shooting a pool game. I'm wearing
the same clothing - I look the same, pretending rather
shadily, yet rather tame. Watch me shoot cleft, then
watch who left. For goodness sakes it's a buzzard
crawling my way - today is the big guys day.

Sequence of faces

Along comes little feather emptying her nest, seeing the
others doing the rest - I freqent the places of tomorrow,
yesterday and evermore. The quiet open places with
a seqence of faces. Lets open the wooden box that we
have upstairs, knowing that nobody cares. But when you
look inside check it twise, cause I think grandma left a
couple of mice and when you see the mice be real nice
cause I think grandma will put you on ice, and when
the kitty comes to play lets make haste. We'll lay a bed
of hay, for the kitty to make nice and lays our chosen
way. Then we will choose his favorite spot and fill with
milk his favorite pot. Then my mice can knaw away
on their favorite rope knot. Another cat and another
mouse and all ends well in this little, little house.

Sweet upon my brow

Oh angel on high I just need to ask why, is it written in his eye. My forever asking, my forever searching - whisper to me in the air oh true and fair, oh angel on high I suckle upon the thorns of past, never forgetting - at last.........
at last. So many times I have asked, why was it purposed that she should die...................oh angel tell me no lie. Sweet upon my brow, sweet it is, sweet, so sweet.

Something in everything and everything in something.
Movements with every turn I make, so let me
reckon with my every mistake while I'm standing
on the corner and considered to be the wreck..
I'm reminded, molded and told to lie, standing in
the middle of a pond of water I wipe my eye.
My reflection is the vision of one another for the rest of my
life, as it all stands still, I tredge all up hill. Preaching and
reaching while my world turns and I'm standing still while
I watch them all burn. Wounded I remain as I am with a
broken wing and no hope for a sling. A master piece I never
was you'd only hear me cuss and cuss. I was not performed
nor on the ice, I was not formed of the dust at a price. If
I were told you found love then I'd be happy beyond the
horizon. Casteth me away my love not far from above.
Hasten quickly oh Lord, I'm at my
end and my end has come.

Suddenly..............

Suddenly.. as suddenly as it was lifted, I was sifted, sifted as peter. Satans tempting... no, I wouldn't even consider to eat with her; to dine on such things - you know what it brings. To bring laughter - no sure stop, but taketh you only to the top - where satan tempteth you. A parable will do, the Lords words will certainly break through. It's you the adversary that I never knew, so now I'm telling you. Depart from me of such things there is no need and of a good hand I do feed. I trust the hand that feeds me, the God I've known - and in spirit and strength I have grown. Still is my heart, I count it as lost. Is this my start, but then again I plead no heart - how are you to shield me and who should challenge thee. I trust in the day that the wave did come, the wall in the moment that inticed me, far beyond the reach of those who thirst. I embrace those tender moments - together we understand, together..... take my hand.

Sonya Johnston

My dear daughter

Would a Lily captivate your beauty my daughter would it depart from you anymore than solomons tent from he. Would a rose assure you my daughter of your fragrance to the Lord, a pleasant fragrance undying to the nostrils. Let the violet with stand all that it is, it's beauty and fragrance be yours my daughter. Let your foot not slip and wound not your hip.

The straws of last

If you come looking don't look hard and don't look
long, I've not gone missing and I'm not really gone.
I'm down on that long winding road carrying my own
load. Come what may - this is the only way and this is all I
have to say, it's been one rainy day along my walk, looking
for some one just to talk. There's no sun on the left and
no sun to the right, just straight ahead I'm grasping straws
to the future and at my diamond shaped heart, there are
four points to no end forfieting any hope of a friend. The
loneliness to my cubic danger hung away like the public
manger. My never ending quest for justice keeps my nest
of hunches - ever growing, and ever knowing splattered
across the solar system with every corner I turn. I see the
politics of my heart ministering to every body part. I make
of myself nothing and nothing shall I make of myself.

Sonya Johnston

The fantacy of my youth where with will it take me-
from yonder, past gone.....those I ponder. Has the Lord
counted the lots set against my heart, cast me not so far
away or my heart will be troubled this day, settle me
not oh Lord and please stay. Let it be a little difficult
to explain, to be truthful and make it plain. If you'll
excuse me, I'll articulate an autistic profile, I'll set it as
a strangers file. Let me not be alone, I really wouldn't
want to experience it - though I'm never really home. I
often sit all alone, if I'm sitting a while.....likely I won't
smile. I like to sit and rock while others like going for
an evening walk. I.....like so many sit in a world of my
demise, meeting often only at the eyes. But somewhere
I've been drowning in my cup of tears.....it's been this
way for years. Remembering the dawn over the girl - that
cloud of doom; I could feel it in every room. It would be
years a- way, they said she couldn't stay, somewhere in
this pulpitating organ called a heart God made the way.

The mind field

The mind field of my thirst, a field
of thoughts the query first.
It's the beginning and it's the end .... for a time, so
just let me pretend. The quest of fulfillment an ardent
response, arduous to my delivery.. it nearly missed me. A
mind field of thirst, I would be the first. A place of rot
and decay - it would be my fussion. Mother May - the
mountains I seek to climb and the valley I dare to cross
in time, my soul has brought forth my own desolation; I
claimed it as a vexation to my contrite heart, and vowed
we wouldn't be long apart. Hear my words oh city of my
troubles - so far I've gone leaving behind a legacy and the
seed of me plucked before her time, not thinking that
she was mine. There is a remnant of her soul in a land
only I know. Ripped and torn and still very worn. I await
that child and I'm amiss... my eyes are steadfast upon one
good night kiss. The message of ones help in a bottle tied
tightly and hand held and the four letter word of my heart
that my very breath spelled. Of forgiveness not known
from far beyond I'd never been shown. It was a cold mid-
night moon, the army would be leaving soon, in a town
lit by fire it was now time to retire. Remembering times
of old and remembering the army that wouldn't be sold.

Pastor

Can you meet me right where I'm at, I mean
meet me in the middle some where.

It may vary

So many find themselves in singlehood while others manage to marry once or twise. From the throne of singlehood to the alter of marriage - many bring with them one large carriage. A carriage of baggage of matrimony and endorsements. A covenant of promises bound for shambles. A park bench made of stone.....
and writings straight from the throne; the suspence played a key part - it was something I didn't really want to start. Perhaps if I could paint 100 pieces to a picture I wouldn't have to set you to find her. I'll go on crying my highway of tears escaping all my years, and trudging forth conquering all my fears. I think of yesteryear and the support beams of what was very near- the closeness of my family I hold very dear. The wine and the water of the family, they comfort me and the bread that kept us fed. The church and the light.....my ever enduring plight. As a member and a unit the measure of our family would be good as we knew it. I remember the host that descended and my loved ones lives that had ended.

Sonya Johnston

To take it in stride

It won't be long before I sing that song, oh victory
I've waited so long. Let not my soul be wrong or my
seed gone and forget not my mother her suffering
was great. In all its stages I still turn the pages.
Let the rocks cry out and let the wicked be in doubt,
allow my suite case to open wide.. an even purpose. I
won't hide, all in all I'll just take it in stride. Let it all
come in, in with the tide, as he spoke up on that hill
with more than pride, he was preachin my fill all about a
land slide. It sorta made me weak when he would speak
and the surprise was in my eyes. Chained and bound to
the thirst of knowledge, a hunger unquenchable. The
thirst I did despies in some of the greatest minds
Within the walls of wisdom.. somebody let me in, so I was
listening - channeling the very essence of the supreme,
I hope you know what I mean as many have never really
seen. My sorrow hits at a high level as the sun sets
down upon me in sole secrecy, I am thankful to thee.
Let your hand console that part of me, left unwhole,
battered and alive - I confide in such an evil pride. I wipe
my watery eyes that are looking up to the skies, setting
over the sun my gain has just begun. I've waited years to
cry these tears, infused with to many fears. Watching their
faces and the faded years, grinding the edge of all my seers.

Self-image

My self-image reflects only my hearts wreck,
shattered as it is.. I harken to things such as
this, my self-image has paved my way.
My righteousness of long lasting has stained my
everlasting. I dreamed that I drew a line and by the
broken wings of a sparrow I took aim with my arrow. I
realized how quaint life would be if only bended on knee.

A troublesome story

He hit her from behind, she didn't see it coming she was blind I heard a troublesome story, some troublesome news, it troubled my soul and even vexed me whole. An art few will find, known only to the dying kind. So lovely in her youth and startling was the truth - soaring through the African Plain, sight seeing and pressing through all kinds of pain. She was alone, I never could known. It's a feeling on my sleeve that I'd rather just leave.

Bitter waters

It's in the enchanted waters that I find the untamed
souls..... the foreaging of bitter waters leaves me thirsting
earthly matters, the living streams of everlasting life
or so it seems.. Pour my cup to over... flowing that
my bitterness not be knowing. The thirsting of the
children of tomorrow, may they never know sorrow.
I say unto you depart from me the broken heart and
escape the broken gate. Spare the rod and spoil the child
these days things are more mild and many children
have grown wild. Oh child of interest, a child like all
the rest, your life was merely a test - live it and be the
best. Take it day by day, but take it all the way. Life
is but a time learn well in your prime, then wisdom
will dress you and always she will see you through.

Destiny.......

Child of destiny if you please, regard me as nothing I'm
a disease. Could I address you in all your hard works.
Answer in prayer, answer in prayer oh answer in prayer. My
secrets please don't share, it's in my doubt that I stare cause
I don't really have a care. Forbid not the blue bird, the blue
jay if I may, I've come more to address him day by day.

A chat with the cat

Talitha - Eve my crazy cat every morning she drinks from my hat, while I'm waiting on her I see that old rugged rat. I stand in second while the rat chats with the cat. I missed the punch line but that's no surprise, now open that mouth and tell me no lies and tell the rat.... no alibis. Now stand somewhere between nothing and making it something and along the breach a lesson I'll teach. I was somewhere on the fence with little less than a thought of suspense. I was engaged in prayer.... that's when I saw my crazy cat. She had a cross around her neck - I swear and booties on her feet, and tease me she did...... then she took her seat.

Ghost of myself

I am a ghost who will not remain still
I am a ghost they can not kill. I seek
answers and come for a thrill, you can
not stop what you can not see. I seek
vengence I will not cease. I am a thief
by night, I come with great fright - I am
the ghost who makes things right, I am
literal.

Sometimes I do

A day of prayer and all is fair
and all the players stop and stare,
I get caught up in the moment of
mounting my mare and it doesn't
really matter,,,,no one will care.....
If the cross didn't stand my life would
be more like an hour glass of sand -
but so well planned that my sight fails
me, never looking behind and never going blind.

It's for real......

I don't know how to tell you how I feel and that this life
is for real. I don't know how to show you how I feel and
often believe it's the real deal - tell me Lord am I for real, I
feel like a child on the cross forsaken by all even the boss.
He forgot to name himself my head and condemned me
instead. I'll wear the cement slabs for you oh Lord - for
I am your child. I'd wear chains and shackles and call
myself wild. I'd marry and happily at that, it would be
for better or for worse and until death do us part and that
day at the alter I gave you my heart. A promise to grow
old together and all sorts of problems we'd weather. We'd
never wonder or stray, forever.........It was the only way, for
better or for worse we'd always stay and until death do
us part. That was the hearty one, so where do I start?

My house

My house was a lot,
rubble and stubble, so
I begin to fumble- the
dishes are in disarray and
have been moved from the
tray. My house was well lit,
funny for a bit I thought as I
stumble through to sit. My
house was my own and didn't
like being alone, so I invited my
family in.

Sonya Johnston

Born in Pembrook Ont, Feb 11, 1967 I was given the name Sonya Morette Renwick, by my father William Howard Renwick and my mother Gail Amy Yates. After living several places in Canada I finally settled my roots in beautiful british columbia, a place that my mother called home and now a place I call home. Over the last 20 years I have finished a writers course, raised a family, finished several biblical courses written several manuscripts and finally became a reverend. But most of all I have wrapped all my love up in my 2 grandsons, Seth and william.

9 780228 873280